The Fairies First Flight

by Trisha Speed Shaskan
illustrated by Jisun Lee

raintree
a Capstone company — publishers for children

KU-168-329

Flick and Flack were best friends.

Flick liked to fan and flutter her wings. She had the finest wings.

Flack's wings weren't as fine as Flick's. He could only flip-flop.

It was Flick and Flack's first year at flying school. On Friday, Miss Freefall asked the fairies, "Are you in tip-top shape?"

"Yes!" the fairies said.

"Fabulous! Then you're almost ready to fly!" said Miss Freefall.

"Fan, flutter," thought Flick.

"Flip-flop," thought Flack.

"First, you need to figure out the magical phrase," said Miss Freefall.

"The phrase is made up of three things. First is the way your wings move. Second is what happens when you say the words fast. And third is the shape you have to be in to fly!"

"Let's figure out the phrase!" the fairies said. Then all of the fairies fled.

Some fairies fled to the kitchen. Some fled down the hallway. Flick and Flack fled to the flower field.

"First, we need to work out the way our wings move," said Flick.

Flack flapped his wings. "Flip-flop," he said.

Flick flapped her wings. "Fan, flutter," she said.

"Now we need to say the words fast," said Flick.

"Flip-flop," said Flack.

"Faster!" said Flick.

14

"Flip-flop, flip-flop, flip-flop," said Flack.

"Flack!" said Flick with a frown. "You're spitting and sputtering!"

"That's it!" said Flack. "It's the second clue. It's what happens when you say the words fast!"

"Fan, flutter, spit, sputter!" said Flick.

"Yes!" said Flack. "Flip-flop, spit, sputter."

And with that, Flick and Flack lifted into the air.
But they fell fast.

"What shape do you have to be in to fly?"
asked Flack.

"Tip-top!" said Flick. "Flying is hard!"

"Flip-flop, spit, sputter, tip-top," said Flack.

"Fan, flutter, spit, sputter, tip-top," said Flick.

Flick and Flack both floated. But they fell fast.

"Fan, flutter," sighed Flick.

"Flip-flop," sighed Flack.

Then together they said, "Spit, sputter, tip-top."

The fairies lifted a few feet, floated and flew! Flick's wings fanned and fluttered. Flack's wings flip-flopped. Flick and Flack felt light as feathers.

20

"That's it!" said Flack. "We needed to fan, flutter *and* flip-flop."

"Fan, flutter, flip-flop, spit, sputter, tip-top! Fan, flutter, flip-flop, spit, sputter, tip-top!" they said.

Flick and Flack flew back inside.

"Fan, flutter, flip-flop, spit, sputter, tip-top! Fan, flutter, flip-flop, spit, sputter, tip-top!" they said over and over.

Miss Freefall nearly fainted. "Flick and Flack, that was fast!" she said.

"We worked together," said Flick.

"Fantastic," said Miss Freefall. "Have fun on your first fairy flight!"

More *Tongue Twisters* from Raintree!

WWW.RAINTREE.CO.UK